Moses Mielziner

The Institution of Slavery Among the Ancient Hebrews

according to the Bible and Talmud

Moses Mielziner

The Institution of Slavery Among the Ancient Hebrews
according to the Bible and Talmud

ISBN/EAN: 9783337740856

Printed in Europe, USA, Canada, Australia, Japan

Cover: Foto ©Andreas Hilbeck / pixelio.de

More available books at **www.hansebooks.com**

THE INSTITUTION OF

SLAVERY AMONG THE ANCIENT HEBREWS,

ACCORDING TO THE BIBLE AND TALMUD,

BY

M. MIELZINER, PH. D.,

Professor of Talmud at the Hebrew Union College, Cincinnati.

THE AMERICAN HEBREW PUBLISHING HOUSE,
THE BLOCH PRINTING COMPANY,
CINCINNATI, O.
1894.

CHICAGO,
178 DEARBORN ST.

SLAVERY AMONG HEBREWS.

By Rev. Dr. M. Mielziner,

PROFESSOR IN THE HEBREW UNION COLLEGE

PREFACE.

This treatise on an important and very interesting branch of Biblical Archæ ology was published in 1859, at Copenhagen and Leipzig, under the title, " Die Verhæltnisse der Sklaven bei den alten Hebræern, nach biblischen und talmudi- schen Quellen dargestellt. Ein Beitrag zur hebræisch-juedischen Alterthums- Kunde, von Dr. M Mielziner." The little work attracted a great deal of atten- tion in Germany, and was very favorably received by several eminent scholars, among others, by the late Dr. J M. Jost, who declared it to be, on the whole, the most satisfactory dissertation on the subject of Hebrew slavery. It has since been quoted in numerous works on the different branches of Biblical Literature and Antiquities, among others, in Oehler's Theology of the Old Testament, and especially in Herbert Spencer's Descriptive Sociology (No. 7). By request of some American scholars and theologians, the late Professor H. I. Schmidt, of Columbia College. New York, furnished an English translation, which was pub- lished in the Gettysburg *Evangelical Review*, vol. xiii. No. li. As both the original German edition and the English translation thereof are out of print, we repub- lish here Prof. Schmidt's translation, in a somewhat revised edition.

THE INSTITUTION OF SLAVERY AMONG THE ANCIENT HEBREWS, ACCORDING TO THE BIBLE AND THE TALMUD.

INTRODUCTION.

§ 1.

The Leading Principles of the Legislation of Moses as Regards Hebrew and Non-Hebrew Slaves.

AMONG the religions and legislations of antiquity none could exhibit a spirit so decidedly averse to slavery as the religion and legislation of Moses ; nor could any ancient nation find, in the circumstances of its own origin, such powerful motives to abolish that institution as the people of Israel. A religion which insists so emphatically upon the exalted dignity of man as a being created in the image of God, [1] a legislation which bases its laws upon that dignity of man, [2] and which enjoins, in all its enactments, not only the highest justice, but also the most tender kindness and the most considerate forbearance, especially toward the needy and the unfortunate; a people, lastly, which had itself pined under the yoke of bondage, and had become a nation only through its deliverance from servitude; all these must have made it their object to abrogate, if possible, the unnatural state of slavery, so degrading to the human being.

At the time of the Mosaic legislation, however, slavery was still too deeply and firmly rooted in the economy of all nations to admit of its complete abolition among the Israelitish nation without serious peril to their domestic affairs. Besides, slavery afforded, within certain restrictions, divers important advantages which could not, under the existing circumstances, be disregarded. For, as the relation of the hired laborer, in other words, labor for wages, had not yet been regulated, the man who, either through his own fault or in consequence of unavoidable misfortunes, had become so poor as to be no longer able to maintain himself and his family, could in no other way procure the necessary support and secure himself against the temptation to steal secretly or to rob forcibly, than by becoming a slave. In the event, however, of such an infringement of the right of property having actually taken place, slavery was, because the earliest constitution of the Israelitish nation knew nothing of punishment by imprisonment, [3] well adapted to serve as a means for punishing the thief who had no property. Hence the legislation of Moses suffered slavery to remain, but endeavored to remove that inhumanity and severity which characterized the institution among other nations, and to prepare the way for the complete abolition of it, in the first instance in favor of members of the Hebrew commonwealth, by so limiting the duration and the conditions of the slavery of a Hebrew, that it scarcely deserved to be called slavery any more. How much the legislator had both the amelioration and the ultimate abolition of slavery at heart, is manifest from the circumstance, not accidental, that the first law which limits the slavery of a Hebrew is found at the very head of all the special provisions (Exod. xxi.) made by the legislation of Moses, and the Decalogue, which forms the groundwork of the entire legislation, mentions slaves in the Fourth Commandment (Exod. xx. 10) and secured to them, whether they were of Hebrew or foreign descent, the rest of the Sabbath.

As he proceeds in unfolding his legislation, the law-giver announces two principles which may be regarded as the guiding spirit of all his enactments concerning slaves.

---

1 Gen. i. 26, 27; v. 1. Levit. xix. 2.

2 Gen. ix. 6. In other passages not expressly declared, but indicated. Cf. Deut. xxi. 23; xxv. 3.

3 Although punishment by imprisonment had become known to the Hebrews in Egypt (Cf. Gen. xxxix. 20; xl. 3, 4; xli. 10; xlii. 19), the use of it is nowhere prescribed by the law of Moses. It is true that imprisonment is historically mentioned in Levit. xxiv. 12, and Numb. xv. 34; but the object of this was not punishment, but the detention of a criminal until sentence could be passed upon him. It is not until the time of the later kings that imprisonment occurs as punishment; but even then it is not the result of a judicial decision, but an arbitrary exhibition of despotic power.

The first of these principles occurs frequently, especially in the laws which enjoin kindness and tender consideration in the treatment of strangers, of the oppressed and the unfortunate, [1] and was regarded as more particularly applicable to slaves. This principle may be stated, in general terms, as follows:

"Israel was once himself a slave in Egypt, and there suffered grievous oppression and severity, from which divine mercy has at last delivered him. Israel should, therefore, not similarly oppress those who are under his authority or in adverse circumstances, but should rather show them mercy and kindness."

While this principle forms the basis of all the provisions which the law makes in favor of slaves, generally whether Hebrews or non-Hebrews, the second principle assigns a still more favorable position to the Israelitish slave. This principle can be expressed thus:

"Israel, since his deliverance from Egypt, has entered the service of God—become his servant. But the servant of the Lord ought not to become the servant of men. Perpetual and real servitude can not, therefore, exist among Israelites, for that would be a virtual denial of the sovereignty of God." [2] Hence the restriction as regards the time during which an Israelite might be kept in servitude, and the rule that he should not, during that period, be treated as a bondman or serf, but as a hireling only. It is true that this second principle accrued directly to the benefit only of a citizen of the Hebrew commonwealth, yet it is certain that in its enforcement the way was already prepared for the total abolition of slavery, not only among the Israelites, but among all nations. For, with the diffusion of the knowledge of God among all nations, these would also be elevated to the dignity of servants of God, and thus the principle, that he who serves God can not become the slave of man, would not only be applied to them, but also be adopted by them. [3] So long, however, as this had not yet taken place, so long as the heathen nations remained in their false relation toward God, and thus recognized for themselves the possibility of their being degraded into a state of bondage to men, the law regarded their slaves as such, and insisted for the time being, only upon the observance toward them of every possible consideration of humanity and kindness.

---

1 Exod. xxii. 20; xxiii. 9; Deut. v. 14, 15; x. 19; xv. 15; xvi. 11, 12; xxiv. 18, 22.

2 Levit. xxv. 42, 55; xxvi. 13.

3 The disposition of Judaism to observe this logical consistency in carrying out the principles of the divine law, appears from the Rabbinical exposition in the Talmud, Tract. Gittin fol. 38 and 39, where it is declared that the Israelitish master is bound to set at liberty his heathen slave, just so soon as the latter had, with his consent, taken part in certain religious exercises. By means of such participation in those religious rites, the slave was, according to the same authority, regarded as having raised himself to the position of a servant of God, and could, as such, no longer remain the slave of a man. In Jebamoth, fol. 46, it is, in like manner, declared to be the meaning and intent of the law, that the slave purchased from a heathen by an Israelite, who, however, has not yet assumed the rights of a master over him, recovers his freedom as soon as he voluntarily receives the ritual bath prescribed for proselytes, and declares his readiness to assume all the obligations of Judaism. Cf. Maimonides H. Issure biah xiii. 11.

§ 2.

General Terms Denoting the Slave-Relation Among the Hebrews.

The most common word of the Hebrew language denoting a slave is עבד (Ebed). But this word, which is derived from the verb עבד (Abad), signifying *to labor, to serve*, denoted originally not merely the actual condition of a slave or serf, but was the common term for all whose position was one of servitude, dependence or subordination. It sometimes even expresses only the notion of moral subordination, sometimes, indeed, nothing more than submissiveness and voluntary compliance with the demands of others: Cf. Prov. xix. 29, 1; Kings xii. 17. Thus then the term עבד (Ebed) was far from signifying a relation so degrading as that which we designate by the word *slave* or *bondman;* on the contrary, the word had often the milder meaning which we, in certain connections, attach to the word *servant*. Thus even the highest officers of State were called עבדי המלך "*Servants of the King*," just as we say "*Ministers of State*," and, indeed, עבד י' "*Servant of God*," is the highest title of honor conferred upon the prophets and upon pious worshipers of God. In conversation with persons of superior rank, the word was also employed as an expression of courtesy, so that the speaker often designated either himself or some third person with the words "thy servant." See Genesis xviii. 3, and other places.[1] It is, therefore, only from the context that we can ascertain whether the word is used to denote a condition of actual servitude, or whether it is to be understood in a figurative sense.

The opposite of עבד (Ebed) is designated sometimes by אדון (pronounced Adohn), frequently in the *pluralis majestatis* אדנים signifying lord, master; at other times by חפשי, which denotes the free or independent man

Terms of more comprehensive meaning than עבד (Ebed), but less frequently used, are such as indicate, at the same time, the manner in which the master obtained possession of his slaves, whether by purchase, or by their being the children of any of his married slaves. Such terms are the following: מקנת כסף also קנין כסף which both denote a servant "*bought with money*." (See Gen. xvii. 12; xiii. 23; Exod. xii. 24; Levit. xxii. 11.) Also יליד בית "*he that is born in the house*," בן בית "*born in his house*" (literally "*son of the house*"), and בן אמה "*the son of the handmaid*" (Gen. xiv. 14; xv. 3; xvii. 23; Exod. xxiii. 12; Levit. xli. 6; Ecclesiastes ii. 7; Ps. lxxxvi. 16; cxvi. 16; Jerem. II. 14).

The female slave was designated by two distinct terms: אמה (Amah) and שפחה (Shiphcha). The latter term, often used as the opposite of גברת (Gbereth) "*mistress*" (Gen. xvi. 4; Ps. cxxiii. 2. Prov; xxx. 23; Is. xxiv. 2), seems to denote a relation more dependent and humble than אמה [2] (Amah). (Cf. I. Sam. xxv. 41; Exod. xi. 5).

---

1 As merely designating the humility of the speaker, or of some third person referred to, in conversation with a person of superior rank, the word seems to have fallen into disuse in later times. At any rate, no such designation occurs in the later books of the Bible except in prayer, or in conversation with men in power. As early as the times of the Talmud the word עבד (Ebed) was looked upon as the grossest insult, which was, in fact, punished with excommunication. הקורא לחבירו עבד יהא בנירוי Kidushin xxviii.

2 אמה seems to be the *general* term for female slave, just as אמתו in Chaldaic, Syriac and Arabic designate nothing more than female slave, whereas שפחה (probably related to

As the Romans used *puer*, and the Greeks *pais*, so also the Hebrews employed, when speaking in a familiar manner, the word נער (naar) "*boy*," "*fellow*," to denote the slave, and it was even applied to old slaves, such as e. g., Ziba (II. Sam. xvi. 1), who was, according to ch. ix. 10, already the father of many children. The corresponding term, נערה (naarah) "*maid*," "*girl*," was used to denote the female slave.

The whole number of slaves belonging to any one master (*the familia* of the Romans) was called עבדה (Abudda). Gen. xxvi. 14; Job. i. 3.

I.—THE CONDITION OF SLAVES OF HEBREW BIRTH.

§ 3.

A. The Hebrew Bondman.

Some have advanced the conjecture that עברי (Ibri), "*Hebrew*," is a term more comprehensive than "*Israelite*," so that the provisions of the law relating to the Hebrew slaves would apply, not only to the Israelitish slaves but to those also who had been obtained from the other nations that had sprung from Abraham, the Hebrew (Gen. xiv. 13), or from *Eber*, the progenitor of Abraham (Gen. x. 21, 24; xi. 16). This notion is already refuted by Ibn Ezra, and justly so (in his comment to Exod. xxi.) by proving, in a general way, from Exod. i. 13; v. 3, and

---

משחה, which occurs only in Hebrew), may have denoted only a certain class of female slaves who performed the meanest menial services of the household, and were under the special control of the mistress of the family (גברת). This may serve to explain why Hagar who, in the sixteenth ch. of Gen. always called שפחה שרי, is subsequently always denominated as אמה. For through the birth of Ishmael she was raised above the degraded condition in which she had stood to Sarah, and became simply אמה. Bilha and Silpa, on the contrary, always remained in their debased relation toward Jacob's two wives, to whom they had been given by Laban, whence they are always (with the sole exception of Gen. xxx. 3, where אמה in the mouth of Rachel, who was still very young, is a mere euphemism) called שפחות (handmaids). The law of Moses, which addresses itself more directly to the male, and has reference, whenever it speaks of female slaves, only to the serving women in general, employs, therefore, always the terms אמתך and אמתו. Once only (Levit. xix. 20) שפחה is used; but it is here emphatic, as it is intended to give prominence to her debased condition, which circumstance distinguishes this case from that in Deut. xxii. 23, 24. In the historical portions of the Bible, whenever it is unnecessary to give prominence to any distinction, particularly when the word handmaid is employed in a figurative sense by a woman to denote submissiveness, both אמה and שפחה are used. It may be observed, however, that (in the plural) שפחות occurs more frequently than אמהות, probably, because there is something anomalous in the latter plural form. It is necessary to note also the usage observed in the Mishna and the Gemara, in which the Hebrew serving woman is, as a rule, called אמה עבריה; the heathen bondwoman, on the contrary, is in every instance called שפחה כנענית. Deviations from this usage, such as those which occur in Baba Mez. i. 5, and Erubin vii. 6. עברו ושפחתו העברים are rare. Saalschuetz. M. R., p. 708, note 911, suggests that "Shiphcha may denote a bondwoman who had not yet been married; Amah, on the contrary, one who had." This theory is confuted by the circumstance mentioned above, that the law always employs the word Amah, and that the only passage in which it makes use of the word Shiphcha (Levit. xix. 20), refers to the case of a married bondwoman.

Jonah i. 9, that עברי denotes only an Israelite, [1] and by appealing, with reference to the Hebrew slave, particularly to Deut. xv. 12, and Jerem. xxxiv. 9, where the law is, by the addition of the words אחיך in the one and יהודי in the other place, expressly limited to the Israelitish slave. Besides these citations, Michaelis (M. R. § 127) adduces Levit. xxv. 44, where the Israelites are authorized to hold slaves for life from among the surrounding peoples. But these peoples were, for the most part, either direct descendants of Abraham or of his brother's son, as, for example, the Ishmaelites, Midianites, Edomites, Ammonites and Moabites. But as no Canaanites were, according to Deut. xx. 16, sqq., to be made slaves, there would, if the above-named peoples were also to be excluded, scarcely any neighboring nation have been left from among whom the regular slaves could be taken. According to the above principle (§ 1), which determined the character of the Mosaic legislation respecting slaves, it is no more to be doubted that by עבד עברי none but the Israelitish slave is meant, since the reason assigned in Levit. xxv. 42, 55, for the treatment he was to receive can have no particular application except to Israelites.

1.—THE HEBREW BONDMAN IN THE SERVICE OF A HEBREW.

§ 4.

a. In What Manner Could a Hebrew Become a Slave?

We have seen above, with what inward repugnance the legislation of Moses permitted, and that for a limited period only, the enslavement of a member of the Hebrew commonwealth; it was therefore quite natural that this permission should be restricted to cases only of extreme necessity. In view of the relations prevailing among the Israelites, but two cases of this description could possibly arise:

1. When a man had been obliged to part with his hereditary possession, and could no longer maintain himself and his family by voluntary or free labor. In order to protect him and his family against extreme destitution and the temptations which would attend it, and perhaps, also, to afford him an opportunity to earn, by serving for several years, what would enable him to redeem the possession which he had sold (Levit. xxv. 26), and thus to re-establish his household, he was allowed to sell himself for a specified time to some rich man as his servant. Levit. xxv. 39.

Considering the love of liberty which the perpetual remembrance of the deliverance from Egypt could not fail to keep alive in the breast of every Israelite, as also the degradation which must have been associated with slavery in the eyes of a people who had been taught in the earliest sacred history (Gen. ix. 25), that it had its origin in a *curse* pronounced upon *moral depravity*—in view of all

---

1 Ewald (Critical Grammar of the Hebrew Language, §4) observes that all the descendants of Eber, hence also the Ishmaelites, the posterity of Esau, etc., should, indeed, call themselves Hebrews, but that, as the collateral lines gradually obtained particular names, the name Hebrew had continued to be pre-eminently the appellative of the direct descendants of Eber through Abraham. As regards the difference between the two names, *Israelites* and *Hebrews*, the same author says (Ib. §3) that Israelite is the religious or sacred name. Hebrews, on the contrary, is the ordinary, vulgar national appelative, which is to be regarded as merely distinguishing the nation from other nations, irrespective entirely of religion.

this the law could take for granted that no man would avail himself of this permission to surrender himself voluntarily into servitude, except only when, in consequence of his extreme destitution, he had no other resource left. [1]

2. When a man had stolen and was unable to make restitution. The object to be attained in this case was not only to restore his property to him who had been robbed, but also to punish the thief when no other punishment was practicable, by at least depriving him for a time of his liberty. Hence the magistrate was to sell him for a time, and from the proceeds of the sale full restitution was to be made for his theft. Exod. xxii. 3.

According to Josephus, [2] the thief was, as a rule, sold to the same man whom he had robbed, and that not only for the simple value of the stolen property, but for the fourfold or fivefold restitution prescribed by the law (Exod. xxii. 1). The Rabbis assert that he could be sold to any other Hebrew, but, at all events, not publicly in the slave market, or "from the stone," and in this case he was sold only for the simple value of what he had stolen, without regard to four or fivefold restitution. [3]

These two cases are the only ones in which the law allowed the sale of a Hebrew. That insolvent debtors also, or their children (as Michaelis, Jahn, Scholz, Ewald and even Saalschuetz maintain), could be made slaves or sold into bondage by the creditor, we most decidedly deny. An arrangement of this kind finds no support whatever in the Mosaic law, nor can the slightest trace of its having existed at any time be found in the Rabbinical tradition. [4] It would, in fact, be utterly irreconcilable with the spirit that pervades all the provisions of the Mosaic law with regard to debtors. That the same law which forbids the creditor to retain over night the garment which his poor neighbor had given in pledge (Exod. xxii. 26, sq.; Deut. xxiv. 12, sq.), or to take as a pledge any necessary household utensil (Deut. xxiv. 6), or even to enter the house of his debtor for the purpose of fetching thence what the debtor had pledged (Ib. xxiv. 10, sq.),—that such a law should give up to the arbitrary disposal of a hardhearted creditor, the body and the liberty of an impoverished debtor or his children, is simply impossible.

It can not, indeed, be denied that in II. Kings iv. 1, and in Nehem. v. 5, we have historical examples, where creditors attempted to reduce the children of insolvent debtors to bondage; but here it is necessary to note to what period those two examples belong. The first occurred during the reign of the house of Ahab in Israel, in which time all the laws of Moses were disregarded; and the second during the period immediately succeeding the return from the Babylonish captivity, when the relations established by law had not yet been regulated.

---

1 What is here simply presumed has been represented by the Rabbis as having the character of a legislative enactment; for they assert that a man was not allowed to sell himself merely for the purpose of gain, but only after he had sold all that he possessed, except his last garment, in order to keep himself from starvation. Maim. H., Abadim I. 2.

2 Ant. IV. 8, 27.

3 Kidushin 18, a. Cf. Maimon. Hilch. Gnevah. III. 12.

4 In the Talmud Tract. Baba Kama 97 a., it is stated, in terms of disapprobation, that some man would have compelled the slaves of his debtor to work. In this place, however, the disapprobation expressed refers in reality to the usurious profit which it was attempted to realize, מיחזי כריבית

In both places, however, the whole tenor of the narrative shows that the proceeding of the creditors was illegal and unjust, having no foundation in any national custom that conferred the right to institute such measures. [1]

The other passages, to which some have referred in order to prove that slavery, on account of unpaid debts, prevailed among the Hebrews, are even still less to the purpose.

If in Prov. xxii. 7, we read: ועבד לוה לאיש מכוה, "*the borrower is servant to the lender*," this is no more to be taken literally than are the words found in ch. xi. v. 29, : עבד אויל לחכם לב, "*the fool is servant to the wise man.*" On the contrary, the word עבד conveys in both places, as in many others, only the notion of dependence in civil society, or a relation of moral subordination toward one who occupies a higher position. The words which occur in the first verse of the fiftieth chapter of Isaiah, where the prophet, speaking in the name of God, says: "Which of my creditors is it to whom I have sold you?" prove no more than this, that the debtor sometimes surrendered objects in his possession, and perhaps even slaves, in the way of sale, to his creditor, instead of paying him the sum of money which was due to him. But the passage by no means proves that the debtor or his children could, without their consent, be taken as slaves by the creditor, or sold by him into bondage. [2]

§ 5.

b. *The Duration of Bondage as Restricted by the Law.*

Inasmuch as the law in the two cases above described, permitted a member of the Hebrew commonwealth to become a bondman, it was necessary, in accordance with the general principle that a Hebrew as a servant of God could not in the proper sense of the word, become a servant of men, that the law should restrict the duration of such servitude, in order that, by means of this restriction, the permitted sale of an Israelite might receive the character of a mere *hiring out* of the person thus sold.

For the accomplishment of this object two periods were appointed, at each of which the Hebrew servant was to recover his freedom without a ransom.

1. The seventh year, counting from the time when he was sold. Exod. xxi. 2; Deut. xv. 12.

2. The fiftieth year, or the year of Jubilee. Levit. xxv. 40.

Ordinarily the Hebrew servant recovered his liberty after six years of servitude, at the beginning of the seventh year, [3] but if it happened that he was sold

---

1 It appears to us that this is indicated already in the word צעקה which occurs in both places (in II. Kings iv. 1, as a verb, and in Nehem. v. 1, as a noun צעקה, as this word frequently denotes a crying out at some grievous wrong endured (Cf. for example, Exod. xxii. 27; Job xix. 7, and especially Isaiah v. 7, לצרקה והנה צעקה).

2 As regards the argument which it has been attempted to derive from Matt. xviii. 25, Kall has already remarked correctly: "Ibi non historia scribitur, sed pingitur parabola eaque fortasse ad mores Romanorum adcommodata, qui pridem in Judaea rerum potiebantur. Apud illos scilicet malae fidei debitores solebant vendi."

3 As the law aimed only at restricting the duration of slavery, it is a matter of course that it did not, with the expression, "six years shall he serve," require that every term of service should, under all circumstances, last the full period of six years; its sole design was to fix the utmost length of time that any term of servitude could continue. It is, therefore,

a few years before the year of Jubilee, he did not wait for the seventh year, but recovered his freedom as soon as the year of Jubilee arrived. [1]

That the seventh year, in which the slave was to recover his liberty, really denotes the seventh year from the time when he was purchased, and not, as some have assumed, the Sabbatical year, is confirmed by the very circumstance that the law, in every instance, mentions only the seventh year, without even em ploying the term " Sabbatical year," and that, in the descriptions of the Sab-

---

also a matter of course, that when a man was sold into bondage a shorter term of service than six years could be stipulated; as e. g., when there was no necessity of a man's servitude lasting more than one or two years. This view of the subject is confirmed by the Rabbis, but only with respect to one who sold himself because of his poverty; according to their opinion, the man who was sold by the judges on account of theft could only be sold for six years, and not for a shorter period. And accordingly, if the value of the stolen property was less than the wages of a term of six years' service, the thief was not sold at all (Cf. Kiduschin 18, a., and Maimonides " Concerning Theft," iii. 14). We may here remark that, according to the dominant view of the most ancient Talmudists, as well as of the later Rabbinical commentators, there was a difference made in the application of the law between the man who was sold by the judges because of his failing to make restitution for theft (הנמכר בג"ד) and him who sold himself on account of poverty (המוכר את עצמו), inasmuch as the provisions of the law recorded, Exod. xxi. 2-6, and Deut. xv. 12, sqq., had reference only to the *former*, whereas the servant who had voluntarily gone into servitude on account of his poverty had been subject to no other rule than that laid down in Levit. xxv. 40, so that the latter might sell himself for a longer period than six years, and *should* not recover his liberty until the year of Jubilee. At an earlier period, however, this opinion was refuted by Rabbi Elieser, who asserts (Kiduschin 14. b.) that the man who went voluntarily into servitude was, by the law, placed in all respects on the same footing as the thief who had been sold by the judges. It appears to us that this view is sustained by the following considerations:

a. There are no intimations whatever given in Exod. xxi. 2-6, and Deut. xv. 12, sqq., that there is, in those passages, reference only to the man who was sold for theft. The expression כי תקנה (if thou buy) which might be supposed to convey an intimation of this kind, proves nothing, since in Deut. xv. 12, כי ימכר ("if * * * be sold, etc.,") is used in the place of it (in like manner as in Levit xxv. 39, ונמכר לך *unto thee*, or rather, the verb being in the *niphal* form, " have sold himself unto thee.")

b. Although Levit. xxv. 39, sq., has, as we admit, more direct reference to the impoverished man who voluntarily accepts the state of bondage, nevertheless, the passage is quite applicable to the man who was sold on account of theft, since even the thief was not sold unless he was too poor to make restitution for what he had stolen.

c. Lastly, the Prophet Jeremiah (xxiv. 13), in referring to the law of Moses, speaks in quite a general way of the emancipation of the bondman after the sixth year of service, without so much as hinting at any difference between the voluntary slave and him whose servitude was compulsory. That all the slaves referred to in that passage as having been kept in bondage beyond the legal term of service should have been such as had been sold on account of theft for which no restitution had been made, is highly improbable.

[1] In this way the provisions specified in Exod. xxi. 2 (resp. Deut. xiii. 12, sq.), and Levit. xxv. 40, mutually complete and elucidate each other, so as to preclude all contradiction as regards the different periods of time at which emancipation took place. In the last-mentioned passage, only the dismission from servitude at the year of Jubilee is spoken of, because that article of the law treats principally of the year of Jubilee; in Exod. xxi. 2 (and Deut. xv. 12), on the contrary, it was more particularly designed to determine the usual time of dismission from bondage, wherefore no mention is made of the liberty which the year of Jubilee brought the slave even before the expiration of his six years' term of servitude.

batical year (Levit. xxv. 1–7, and Deut. xv. 1), not a word occurs about the emancipation of slaves.

The limitation of the term of service to six years, and the establishment of the seventh year as the year in which slaves must be set at liberty, are enactments which, as has been remarked already by Arbabanel, and also by Ewald, have an obvious connection with the notion of the Sabbath and of the Sabbatical year. [1] For, in the same manner as the weekly Sabbath should, after six days' labor, and the Sabbatical year, after six years' labor in the field, serve to remind men of the Creator and Ruler of the world, who had allotted to man the cultivation and the productions of the soil, so the emancipation of the slave in the seventh year after a six years' term of servitude was designed to keep both the master and the slave in mind of the sovereignty of God, whose servants both of them were. In Levit. xxv. 42, this commemorative character of the emancipation connected with the year of Jubilee is expressly mentioned. And besides, the emancipation is, in that passage, distinctly connected with the other injunctions regarding the year of jubilee, the design of which obviously was, to restore the original equality of all the members of the Israelitish commonwealth as regards both property and liberty.

§ 6.

c. *Extraordinary cases, in which the Slave obtained his liberty.*

Besides the seventh year of servitude and the year of Jubilee, there were other circumstances in which, as the Rabbis affirm, the Hebrew slave could obtain his liberty. These were:

1. By restoring the purchase money for which he had not yet rendered adequate service; for as soon as the bondman, during his term of service, came, by inheritance or otherwise, into the possession of property, and was thus enabled thereafter to maintain himself by his own resources, as well as to render the required restitution for the theft which he had committed, he could immediately obtain his liberty, even though his master was not willing, by restoring the money which had been paid for him, after deducting as much as would afford him suitable wages for such time as he had already been in servitude. Kiduschin 14b, Maimon. Abad. II., § 8.

2. By his master voluntarily bestowing upon him a certificate of emancipation, in which he renounced all claim to the further services of that slave and to the restoration of the purchase money. Maimon. ibid. § 11.

---

1 Michaelis (Mosaisches Recht) assumes that the law, in prescribing the liberation of the slave in the seventh year, had based that provision upon a custom which prevailed already among the patriarchs and their kin, inasmuch as Jacob had twice served with Laban, and each time for seven years. In the case of Jacob, however, the term of service is seven years, while the law prescribes only six. It is true that in a reference to the Mosaic law which we find in Jerem. xxxiv. 14, the expression מקץ שבע שנים תשלחו ("*At the end of seven years let ye go*") occurs, but the words ועבדך שש שנים ("*And when he hath served thee six years*"), which are immediately subjoined, plainly show that "*seven years*" is here to be taken as a whole, so that we must translate with Philippson: "At the end of a septennium" (or a period of seven years), that is in the seventh year; for the beginning of the last year of a period consisting of several years may be appropriately designated as the end of that period. Cf. Nachmanides and Abarbanel on Deut. xv. 1.

3. By the master's death occurring before the term of service expired without his leaving a son to inherit his property; for the Hebrew servant was under no obligation to serve out his time to any other heir of his deceased master, except his son. Maimon ibid, § 12.

§ 7.

d. *Slavery prolonged beyond the legal term by boring the ear.*

If the Hebrew slave, from attachment to his master or to one of his female slaves with whom he had lived in wedlock, or to the children whom he had by her, did not wish to make use of his liberty, to which he was entitled at the expiration of his six years' term of service, the law allowed him to remain in bondage; but, in order to guard against any abuse of this privilege, and perhaps also by way of punishment for the rejection of the liberty that was offered, ordained as follows : [1]

The slave was, first of all, to be brought before the judges, that he might declare his intention in their presence. It was probably their duty to direct his attention to the consequences of his purpose, and to satisfy themselves that this had not been lightly adopted, or in any way forced upon him by his master. If the slave persisted in his determination, he was to receive, in an exposed, but at the same time the least sensitive part of his person, a mark as a perpetual memorial of his resolution; and for this purpose the boring of the ear, which was also among other nations a sign of servitude, was peculiarly adopted. [2] The master himself performed the process of boring, and this he was to do by boring the ear of the slave against the door-post of his house with an awl, [3] whereby on the one hand, the transac-

---

1 Exod. xxi. 5, 6; Deut. xv. 16, 17.

2 As a mark of bondage, the piercing of the ear is mentioned with reference to the Mesopotamians (Juven. I., 104), the Arabs (Petron. sat. 102), and the Lydians (Xenoph. Anab. III. 1, 31). According to Knobel (Exod. p. 214), the mark denotes that he who wears it has hearing ears, and is, therefore, to be attentive and obedient. Cf. Ps. xl., 6. It is met with, also, among other nations, without being exactly a mark of bondage, but merely as a sign that the person belongs, in a general way, or is devoted, to some other, *e. g.*, as a mark of those who belong to some saint and are his devotees. Cf. Rosenmüller, Morgenland, II., p. 70, sq. Knobel conjectures that in the passage above cited from Exodus the *right* ear is meant, which had the preference in certain acts of purification and consecration. The same thing is affirmed, and for the same reason, by the Talmudists (Kiduschin, 15, a.). The latter, who regard this boring of the ear as exclusively a *punishment* for the rejection of liberty, suggests the following ingenious explanation of the subjection of the ear to this process : Why is the ear just selected for punishment? Because with the ear man has heard the words : "I am thy God, who hath delivered thee from Egypt," and yet has afterwards gone and made himself, a being whom God had made free, the slave of a man; and, therefore, shall the punishment be inflicted upon his ear. In like manner they represent the door post against which the ear was bored, as a memorial of the deliverance from Egypt. (Ibid. fol. 22b.)

3 That this boring was to take place, not only *at* the door, but also *against* it (*unto it*), is plain from Deut. xv. 17. Ibn Esra and Abarbanel understand by הדלת (the door) the city gate where the judges sat. But then the proper word would be השער and not הדלת. And besides, when this law is repeated in Deut. xv. 17, there is no mention whatever of the judges; hence in that place, the gate of justice is not at all to be thought of in connection with ברכת. Ewald (Antiquities, p. 245) understands by הדלת "the door of the sanctuary (because he considers האלהים "the judges to signify a *supreme court* composed of priests, presided over by the high priest and holding its sessions in the sanctuary). In that case, however, both master and slave would have been obliged first to make a pilgrimage to the sanctuary, and this is scarcely implied in והגישו—and he (his master ארניו) shall bring him.

tion was made more public, while on the other hand, also, it was symbolically inti-
mated to the slave, that, whereas he was already *standing on the threshold of liberty,*
he now remained, by his own resolution, *bound as slave to that house.* The dis-
grace and degredation connected with the whole of this transaction, and with the
indelible mark of bondage which the slave was thus perpetually to bear at his ear,
must, if the last spark of self-respect had not become extinct within him, have
deterred the slave from consenting to such a prolongation of the legal term of
his bondage; and this was probably all that the law designed to effect by that
ordinance. [1]

The rabbis call a slave whose ear has thus been bored, נרצע, "one who has
been bored"

According to the natural signification of the expression, ועבדו לעולם " And he
shall serve him forever" (Exod. xxi., 6), as well as this other, והיה לך עבד עולם
" *and he shall be thy servant forever"* (Deut. xv, 17), the slave who had received
that mark, remained to the end of his life in the service of his master. In this
sense the passages are understood by most of the more recent exegetical commentators of the Scriptures. The rabbinical tradition, [2] on the contrary, and also
Josephus [3] understand לעולם ("for ever") to mean "till the time of the year of
Jubilee," so that the slave who had his ear bored recovered his liberty at all events
in the year of Jubilee, forasmuch as, according to Levit. xxv. 10, that year was to
restore liberty to all Hebrew inhabitants of the land. [4]

---

1 It is probable that this ordinance was never carried into effect; at any rate this was
scarcely practicable, if all the numberless conditions which tradition (Kidushin 22a and
Mechiltha and Siphri) represents as indispensable to the execution of it, had really to be observed.

2 Kidushin fol. 14 and 15.

3 Antiquities iv. 8, 28.

4 In order to vindicate the correctness of the traditional rendering Ibn Esra observes that
עוים frequently denotes only a *period of time.* To the argument in favor of this which he de-
rives from Eccles. i. 10. כבר היה לעולמים (" it hath been already of old time "), and from L.
Sam. i. 22, וישב שם עד עולם) " and there abide forever"), Munk (Palestine page 141) adds
another still more striking from Is. xxxii, 14 and 15 where upon עד עולם (in aeternum) a limiting עד (donec) follows. But as time was among the Israelites divided into jubilee-cycles,
the opening upon a new jubilee-cycle could be appropriately designated by עוים. In connection with Exod. xxi. 6, Philippson makes the remark, that the word עוים " has been chosen in
this place only because the year of Jubilee was instituted at a later period." But when he
alleges this reason, the question still remains, why a similar expression is afterwards again
employed in Deut. xv., 17, subsequently to the institution of the year of Jubilee. To the traditional interpretation of the passage Saalschutz (d. Mos. Recht, 699) urges this among other
objections: " I can not comprehend how the year of Jubilee should, without any intimation
of this sort from the legislator, bestow upon the slave the right previously denied him, to take
with him the bondwoman who belonged to the master, and also her children; and without this
emancipation would surely have had no attractions for him." Another objection is made by
Knobel, Exod. page 214, " the declaration of the slave that he does not wish to become free
shows, that in this case perpetual bondage is meant." But there is here one thing to be considered, which bears forcibly against these two objections, and that is, that in the year of
Jubilee every Israelite was to be repossessed by his paternal estate (possession) which he had
sold. In possession of this now unincumbered paternal estate the man who had hitherto been
a slave could not possibly be willing any longer to forego his liberty, which in times past he
had relinquished solely under the pressure of circumstances; and what is more, he was, by

According to the views of Talmudists, the slave who had his ear bored was to obtain his liberty, not only in the year of Jubilee, but also at the death of his master, since he could be inherited neither by the son nor by any other relative. [1]

§ 8.

e. Position and Treatment of the Hebrew Slave During His Bondage.

By restricting the duration of servitude to a term of years, the Mosaic law has repudiated the principle of slavery and converted the sale of a Hebrew into a mere hiring out of the man for a limited time; but, in accordance with this, it actually requires that his condition simply be that of a hired servant, and that, as such, he has to be treated with kindness and with all due consideration (Levit. xxv. 40, 42, 43).

It was only the time and labor of the purchased Israelite that belonged, during the term of servitude, to the master, not, however, his *person* or his *property*. And accordingly the master had no right to transfer his Hebrew servant to any other person, either by selling or giving him away. [2] If the servant was married when his term of service commenced, the master had no claim whatever to the services of either his wife or children, although he was under obligations to provide for their support. [3] Nor could the master lay claim to anything which the servant, during his term of servitude, might happen to find or to acquire in any other way than by his labor. [4]

As regards the work to be done by the servant, the master could require such only at his hands as he had been accustomed to while he was free. He had no right, under any circumstances, to compel him to perform any of those menial duties which were exclusively obligatory upon real slaves: such, *e. g.*, as attending the master to the bath, and carrying his garments, tying or unfastening his sandals, washing him, anointing him, or carrying him in a sedan-chair. [5] While he was employed in such labor as he might be legally required to do, the servant's physical abilities were to be duly considered, and he was to be allowed

thus recovering his property, in most instances enabled to purchase the freedom of the bond-woman with whom he had lived in contubernio, and that of the children whom she had borne him. And that all this is really assumed by the law is plain from this circumstance alone, that with reference to the Year of Jubilee it does not at all take into account, as it does in its provisions for emancipation at the end of a six years' servitude, the contingency of any slave, not desiring to avail himself of the liberty to which he had a legal claim.

1 The Talmud (Kidushin 17, 6) deduces this rule from literal explanation of the suffix in וֹעֲבָדוֹ " *let him serve him*," *him*, the master only, but not an heir לוֹ וְלֹא לְיוֹרְשָׁיו.

2 Maim. Abad. iv. 10.

3 Kidushin 22 and Maim. Ibid. iii. 1, 2.

4 Mishna Baba Mezia, i. 5.

5 All these specifications are based upon the injunction of the law, in Levit. xxv. 39. " thou sha't not compel him to serve as a bondservant." It is interesting here to note that those menial services, mentioned above, could be legitimately required of a *free* Israelite who had hired himself out as a day laborer; and this is accounted for by the Rabbis on the ground that such a one had, of his own accord, consented to do such work, whereas the purchased servant has less opportunity of exercising his free will, and is, therefore, more liable to be degraded by humiliating services.

the necessary rest and recreation.[1] Although the servant was bound to be always obedient and submissive to his master, the latter was not allowed to make him feel his dependent condition, to chastise him, or to hurt his feelings with harsh words, but was always to treat him with friendliness and fraternal kindness.[2] If he had injured him by means of a blow, the servant was entitled to the same indemnification which the law provides for an injury done to a free citizen.[3] The food, clothing and dwelling to which the servant was entitled, were to correspond with the pecuniary circumstances of the master.[4]

In one particular only the Hebrew servant was the same as the real slave not belonging to the Hebrew commonwealth; and this was, that, according to Exod. xxi. 4, the master could give him one of his female slaves[5] as a wife for the whole term of his servitude. This union was not regarded as a civil marriage sanctioned by religion (קידושין Kidushin), but only as a contubernium (Kidushin 68), and the children who were born in a union of this kind belonged, as "born in the house," to the master, and did as little go with the bondman when he became free as did the mother.[6]

---

1 Maim. Ibid. i. 6.

2 Ibid. § 9

3 Mishna Baba Kama viii. 3. The Rabbis justly regard the provisions of the law in Exod. xxi. 26, 27, as having reference only to non-Hebrew slaves, as the Hebrew servant became free, at any rate, after the sixth year of service, or at the year of Jubilee, so that his immediate emancipation would have afforded no adequate indemnification for any serious injury that he might have sustained.

4 The Rabbis, in their exposition of the law, go, we presume, too far, when they say that under no circumstances were the food, clothing and dwelling of the servant to be inferior to those of the master; whence the proverb arose: "He that has bought a Hebrew slave, has, as it were, bought himself a master." Kidushin, 22.

5 The Rabbis rightly assume that a bondwoman from among a heathen people is here meant; for the Hebrew maid-servant became free, as well as the man-servant, after the sixth year of service, so that it could not be said of her, "the wife and her children shall belong to her master." Salvador (Histoire des Institutes de Moise, livre vii. ch. v), and also Bertheau (Sieben Gruppen mos. Gesetz, p. 22), are of opinion that reference is here made to a Hebrew bondwoman, who had entered into servitude later than the bondman, so that, at the time when the latter obtained his liberty, she would still have to remain with the master until she had served out her six years. But then what interest could the master have had in giving his Hebrew servant such a female slave as a contubernalis, if he had been obliged to set her, together with her children, at liberty in the course of a few years, before he could derive any profit from these children? That, in such a case, the children would have to go with the mother when the latter recovered her liberty, can not be doubted.

6 Michaelis (Mos. Recht. § 127, Note) has propounded the question, whether these children of a father who was at the time a slave did not, at all events, according to Levit. xxv. 41, obtain their liberty in the year of Jubilee. But whilst he does not venture to express himself positively upon this subject, Phillipson (die Israelite. Bible. pp. 424 and 425) assumes the emancipation of these children in the year of jubilee as a matter of course. Even Josephus is, perhaps, of the same opinion. He says: (Antiq. iv., 8, 28) of the slave who was living in contubernio, that he obtained his liberty in the year of Jubilee, and adds: "taking away with him his children and his wife, they also to be free." In decided opposition to these opinions are the views of the Talmudists (Kidushin 68 and 69), according to whom such children are to be regarded as absolute slaves, inasmuch as they shared the condition of the mother (וירדיה במלהה), whereas by the children referred to in Levit. xxv. 41, who went with the father when he became free, those only could be meant whom a *free* woman, his wife, had borne

§ 9.

f. *The Gift at Parting.*

At the time of his emancipation, after his six years' term of service, and also, as the Rabbis teach, when he obtained his liberty in the year of Jubilee, the Hebrew servant was not to be permitted by his master to go away empty-handed, but the latter was to bestow upon him a bountiful gift in sheep, grain and wine (Deut. xv. 13, 14). The extent of this gift is not defined by the law, but was to depend upon the pecuniary circumstances and the goodwill of the master. The Rabbis, however, state the minimum value at thirty shekels (Kidushin 17). This emancipation-present had, obviously, a two-fold design. It was to furnish the emancipated slave the means of again establishing his own household, that he might not be compelled, by want, immediately again to sell that liberty which he had just recovered, so that, as the Talmudists declare, [1] the creditors of the slave could not make good any alleged claim to this emancipation-present. But as the slave was not to be compelled, by severity, to perform his duties, this gift was, doubtless, also designed to stimulate him to exert himself during his term of service to deserve the entire satisfaction of his master, as the amount of the gift depended upon the degree to which the latter was satisfied with him. [2]

§ 10.

g. *An Ancient Custom connected with the Discharge of the Slave in the Year of Jubilee.*

The slave's discharge from bondage after his six years' term of service, which took place, of course, as regards individual slaves, at different times, respectively as their terms of servitude had commenced, proceeded quietly and without any particular formalities, but it is natural that with the general emancipation of all Hebrew slaves in the year of Jubilee certain solemnities and formalities should be connected. With regard to this, the law itself prescribed that at the beginning of the year of Jubilee, on the *tenth* day of the seventh month, the

---

him, and who had become slaves at the same time with himself. And it is, perhaps, to these children only that the words of Josephus have reference, especially as he mentions, besides the children, the wife also, by which term he is not likely to designate the bondwoman spoken of above.

1 Kidushin fol. 166 : לו ולא כבעל חובו

2 Those of the Talmudists who, as was observed above (note to § 5) regard the six years' term of service, and hence, also, the boring of the ear when the term was to be prolonged, as well as the cohabitation with one of the master's Canaanitish bondwomen, as referring only to the slave who had been sold on account of theft, hold, as consistency requires them to do, that the law prescribing the parting gift applies, in like manner, only to the slave, whilst the voluntary slave could advance no claim to such a present. They may have been led to this view of the subject by the consideration that the voluntary slave would be able, after recovering his freedom, to employ the purchase-money paid for him in the re-establishment of his own independent household, whereas in the case of the other slave the purchase-money was appropriated as an indemnity for the theft which he had committed. We have shown above, however (note to § 5), that the opposite view held by Rabbi Eliezar, who denies that any difference whatever existed between the voluntary slave and the slave sold on account of theft, is probably correct.

restoration to liberty of all Israelites living in servitude should be proclaimed, with the sound of the trumpet, throughout the land (Levit. xxv. 9, 10). Tradition makes mention of an ancient custom, according to which slaves were discharged from their servile relations as early on the first day of the above-mentioned month, without, however, being as yet dismissed to their homes. During the interim they united in celebrating, in joyous banquets and entertainments, the termination of the servitude; on these occasions they wore garlands on their heads. And when, on the day of Atonement, the trumpet sounded, they returned to their possessions and their families. [1]

2.—The Hebrew Bondman in the Service of a Master who was not a Hebrew.

§ 11.

In cases of necessity the Law (Levit. xxv. 47–55) even allowed the Israelite to sell himself to a man not a Hebrew, provided that he lived in the country and was subject to the laws of the land. [2] In the service of such a master, however, the Hebrew servant could claim, neither his liberty at the end of the sixth year of service, nor the gift bestowed on others at their discharge. For this reason the Israelite, who was compelled by circumstances to accept a state of bondage, must have preferred to sell himself, if possible, to a member of the Hebrew commonwealth, from whom he could in general expect more considerate treatment. But in the year of Jubilee even the slave of one, not a Hebrew, obtained his freedom. But as, during so protracted a term of service in the house of a heathen master the religious faith and the moral character of an Israelitish servant was exposed to danger, [3] the law determined in his favor not only that he should, in case he had acquired property in the meantime, have the privilege of purchasing his own freedom, but also that near or distant relatives should be permitted to release him from his servitude by paying the required ransom [*Vide infra*]. But in order that the master might neither, by exorbitant demands, throw obstacles in the way of such a redemption or render it utterly impossible, nor suffer in his own rights and interests by the discharge of the slave being demanded for an inadequate ransom, [4] the law expressly requires that the amount of the price of redemption shall be strictly proportionate to the purchase-money, and determined according to the number of years of service already expired. Thus, for example, if a man who had sold himself ten years before the year of Jubilee for forty shekels, was to be redeemed after three years of his term of service had expired, then the price of redemption amounted, after twelve shekels had been deducted for the time that he had served, to twenty-eight shekels.

The kinsman who redeemed a slave in this way, did not, by so doing, acquire any claim to the service of the person redeemed. On the contrary, such redemption was looked upon as a duty obligatory upon a man's relatives, a duty which they could, under certain circumstances, even be compelled to perform. [5]

---

1 Talmud Rosh Hashana fol. 8*b*.

2 Cf. Kid. 16*a* : בני שישנו תחת ידיך

3 Cf. Kid. 20*b*. כי היכי דלא ישמע בין הנכרים

4 Cf. Rashi on Levit. xxv. 48.

5 Maimonid. Abadim ii. 7.

The position of the Hebrew servant in the house of a master who was not an Israelite did not essentially differ from that in the house of a fellow-countryman. He was to be regarded as only a hired servant, and to be treated as such with all kindness. As respects the *Hebrew* master, it was only necessary to make this kind treatment dependent upon the dictation of his own conscience : "thou shalt not rule over him with rigor, but shalt fear thy God (Levit. xxv, 43) ; with reference to the heathen master, on the contrary, it is said (ib. v. 53) : He "shall not rule with rigor over him *in thy sight*," which words, as explained by the Rabbis, ordain, that the *magistrates* are to see to this kind treatment. The inference of the magistrates was admissible, however, only when the master's rigor and want of consideration were *clearly manifest.* [1]

B.   *The Hebrew Maid-servant.*

§ 12.

With reference to the bondwoman the Mosaic law displays even a much more tender solicitude than in the case of the Hebrew bondman. Besides the indulgent consideration which it constantly exhibits in view of the depressing circumstances connected with the dependent condition and the loss of liberty of any human being, there was, in the case of the female slave, this additional circumstance to consider, that in a state of servitude a maiden's virtue was more than ordinarily exposed to temptations and to the wiles of seducers. This was especially the case, if the maiden had, at a tender age, been sold by her father because of his poverty, [2] her budding youth and her weakness and inexperience aggravating the dangers which threatened her virtue. That this danger might be removed, the law provides that the master, when purchasing such a maiden, taci'ly assumes the obligation to marry her when she has arrived at the age of puberty, or, at the least, to take her as his concubine.· It is, as a general thing, inconceivable that any fa·her could, except solely in view of such an arrangement, be induced by his destitute condition to sell his daughter. Viewed in this light, the particular specifications in Exod. xxi. 7-11, become perfectly clear, as the following considerations will show :

If the master manifested a willingness to fulfil the tacitly assumed obligation, the maiden was not to go out free, "*as the men-servants do,*" i. e., after the sixth year of service or in the year of Jubilee, as she was no longer to be regarded as a common maidservant, but rather, in a certain sense, as the *betrothed* of the master (v. 7). But if the master showed by his conduct that it was not his intention to marry her or to make her his concubine, he was to concede to her father or to some other member of her family, the privilege of immediately redeeming her, [3]

---

1 Maimon Abadim, i. 6.

2 Only at a tender age (whilst still a minor) could a maiden be sold by her father against her will. When she had arrived at the age of puberty his paternal authority over her ceased, and could be exercised only in a sort of surveillance over her until she was married.

3 This is the most natural sense of והפדה, which has in the Hiphil form a causative signification "to permit to be redeemed." To us it is quite incomprehensible how Ewald (p. 246, note) can claim for the Hiphil form of פדה [to set free] without any authority whatever, the signification "*to marry,*" i. e., to take as concubine," so that והפדה wou'd be only a tautology of יערה [hath betrothed her] and still belong to the connecting clause.

and, as the rabbis affirm, to facilitate her redemption by not demanding full restitution of the purchase money, and by deducting from this the amount that was covered by the services already rendered. [1] But the deceitful master had no right to sell her to a stranger as a maidservant or a concubine (v. 8).

If he did not wish to marry her himself, he could give her to his own son only. In this case, however, he was to "*deal with her after the manner of daughter*," i. e., he was to give her the same dowry as if she were his own daughter, and the son was to treat her as he would any free woman who had become his wife.

But if either the master or his son who had married her, took besides her, another wife, the first one was not to suffer in consequence thereof any diminution of her rights, for he was not allowed to diminish her food, her raiment, and her duty of marriage (v. 10).

But if, when she had arrived at the age of puberty, the master refused either to marry her himself, or to give her to his son, or to effect her redemption, she obtained her liberty at once, without money, and without waiting for the seventh year of service, or the year of Jubilee. [2]

Without the consent of the maiden neither the master nor son could take her to wife. But when such a marriage was contracted the marriage gift customary in other cases was not required, for the reason that the purchase-money paid to the maiden's father was regarded as such. In all other respects this sort of marriage was just as much legally binding and just as sacred as the ordinary marriage, and could, like this, be dissolved only by the husband's death or by a bill of divorce [3]

Of course, however, instances might occur in which the elevation of the purchased maidservant to the position of the master's or the son's wife was entirely out of the question, and in which, moreover, all apprehensions of any dangers threatening her virtue were needless; as, for example, when a Hebrew woman, no longer young, sold herself in consequence of her destitution as a servant for work. In this case the maid-servant was (according to Deut. xv. 14, 17) put on the same footing with the Hebrew man-servant as regards the time for the restoration to liberty, and the gift to be received at the time of parting. [4]

---

1 Kidushin 14*b*.

2 So the Rabbis understand v. 11, vid. Rashi on this verse; Cf. also Maimonides Abad. iv, 9. Others (Rosenmuller, Philippson, Ewald, etc.) refer שלש אלה to the three things mentioned in the preceding verse: שארה כסותה ועונתה which seems, however, less suitable, as it is scarcely proper to say: עשה שארה or עשה כסותה and the like, so that, in the place of לא תעשה לה one ought rather to look for לא יתן לה or יגרע לה. In this verse, moreover, the presumption is no longer admissible that either the master or his son had really taken the maiden to wife, since this event would as a matter of course, have already terminated her state of bondage; upon which supposition, therefore, the words ויצאה חנם אין כסף [" and she shall go out fr.e without money "] would now be quite inappropriate.

3 Maimonid. Abad. iv. 7 and 10.

4 This statement enables us to reconcile, in the most natural manner, the seeming contradiction between Exod xxi. 7 and Deut. xv. 12, 17. For the former passage refers to the special case of a father selling his daughter as a maid-servant, which took place, as a general thing, only on the presumption that the master would either take her himself, or give her to his son, as a wife. The passage in Deuteronomy, on the contrary, has reference to the purchase of a Hebrew woman as a common maid for work, in which case there was no such presumption. Cf. Hengstenberg, the authenticity of the Pentateuch, ii., p. 438, sq. That He-

According to tradition, a Hebrew woman was never sold into slavery on account of a theft she had committed. [1] The ordinance respecting the boring of the ear for the purpose of prolonging the term of service, had also, according to the opinion of the Rabbis, no application to the Hebrew maid-servant. [2] As the Hebrew maid-servant could form no matrimonial union with a slave, there existed, as a general thing, no reason why she should have her term of service prolonged beyond the period fixed by the law. In her case, moreover, a pierced ear could not be a disgraceful mark of slavery, for in ancient times the female sex, as a rule, had the ears bored for the purpose of inserting ornaments. And lastly it may have been looked upon as irreconcilable with a sense of propriety to permit an operation so public and degrading to be performed upon the person of a woman.

The Final Abrogation of Slavery as Respects Members of the Hebrew Commonwealth.

§ 13.

It can not be accurately determined how long and to what extent the laws of Moses regarding the condition of Hebrew slaves were actually carried into effect. That slaves received, upon the whole, that kind treatment and those favors which the law claimed for them, we may safely infer from the silence of the prophets, as these guardians and defenders of all who were oppressed or suffered wrong would certainly not have failed to rebuke any open offenses against those provisions of the law. Only the ordinance respecting the emancipation at the end of six years had, as we learn from the prophet Jeremiah (xxxiv. 14), toward the end of the old Jewish monarchy, for a long time already fallen entirely into disuse. Nor is it difficult to account for the disregard of this particular ordinance. With a tender consideration for certain relations the law itself had allowed the term of service to be prolonged beyond the period of six years. It is natural that the richer Hebrews found it to their interest to make an extended use of this concession, and to induce their Hebrew servants by alluring promises to consent to the prolongation of their term of service. The notice to the judges which the law prescribed to prevent this abuse was probably omitted in most cases, as the master had reason to apprehend that the slave would permit himself to be deterred from persisting in his purpose by the caution of the judges

---

brew women were actually employed in the sole capacity of working slaves, appears from Jerem. xxxiv. 9–12. The Mishna likewise seems evidently to take it for granted in several places (Baba Mezia i., 5; Erubin vii. 6; Maasar Scheni iv. 4, in which last passage the use of שפחה instead of the more usual term אמה must not be overlooked) that Hebrew women who had become of age could also be held as servants. Quite a different view, however, is taken of this subject by the Gemara (Baba Mezia 12, b, Gittin 64b).

1 Mishna Sota iii. 8; Cf. also Maimonid. Abad. i. 2.

2 Kidushin 17, b; Cf. also Maimonid. ib., 13. Philippson, who in general shows a due respect for the traditional acceptation, maintains in opposition to it (p. 424), that the Hebrew maiden could, by having her ear bored in public, remain in service longer; and he endeavors to support his view by an appeal to Deut. xv., 17. The traditional view, however, refers the words ואף לאמתך תעשה־כן in that place ("and also unto thy maid-servant thou shalt do likewise") to verse 13, and thus considers verses 16 and 17 down to עולם (for ever) as a parenthesis. This acceptation of the passage under consideration is, as it appears to us, sustained by the following verse (v. 8), which quite obviously refers back, in like manner, to verse 13.

and by the degradation connected with the boring of his ear. In this way the law of Moses, which restricted the servitude of a Hebrew to a term of six years, fell gradually so completely into oblivion that servants were, even against their will, retained in bondage, because the opinion had come to be entertained that masters had a justly-acquired right to the unlimited services of persons whom they had once bought as slaves. Even in the political reform which was undertaken in the spirit of the Mosaic law by the pious king Josiah, the reintroduction of the ordinance relating to the liberation of slaves after a servitude of six years seems not to have been undertaken, as it was probably presumed that an attempt of this kind would lead to no permanent results. It must, however, have appeared easier and at all events more in accordance with the spirit of the Mosaic legislation, to abolish slavery, entirely, as regards members of the Hebrew Commonwealth, and to introduce labor for wages, or the plan of employing day laborers in its place. An attempt of this kind seems to have been actually made even before the downfall of the old Jewish monarchy. For at the time when Nebuchadnezzar began the siege of Jerusalem, King Zedekiah proposed, probably upon the advices of the prophet Jeremiah, at a popular assembly convened in the temple for the purpose of determining upon a day of humiliation and prayer in view of the impending danger, that every man should let his Hebrew slave and his Hebrew bondwoman go free, and that no man should thereafter hold in bondage a fellow-countryman and fellow-believer. [1]

Both the princes and the people assented to the proposed measure, and the resolution which was adopted by a solemn ceremony was immediately carried into effect. But scarcely was the threatened danger supposed to have passed away, when the rich and powerful repented of what they had done, and again brought their emancipated slaves by force under the yoke of bondage. It was not until the complete overthrow of the ancient monarchy emphatically predicted by the prophet in consequence of this breach of faith, that the slavery of fellow-members of the Hebrew commonwealth really came to an end. An attempt, which was made after the return from the Babylonian captivity, to introduce it again, was energetically crushed by Nehemiah (Nehem. v. 5–10). After that there were in the re-established Jewish commonwealth none but *non-Hebrew* or *heathen slaves*, of whose condition we shall speak in the next sections. Such slaves were held by the Jews who dwelt in Palestine and other oriental countries, even after the downfall of the second Jewish monarchy. The privilege of holding a Hebrew as a slave was regarded as having ceased with the abolishment of

---

1 Vid. Jerem. xxxiv, 8, sqq. The assumption that this emancipation was nothing more than a measure dictated by danger, "so that the number of combatants might be increased in the same manner as it was occasionally done among other nations, by means of emancipated slaves," is sufficiently refuted by the circumstance, that the emancipation was to embrace also the *bondwomen*, whom it was scarcely intended to employ as soldiers. The solemn manner in which the King's proposition was sanctioned at the temple (vv. 15, 18 and 19) indicates on the contrary, that the emancipation was to be an expiatory measure to avert the divine wrath provoked by the enslavement of Hebrew citizens. That the proposition aimed at the *perpetual* abolitiion of the slavery of Hebrew citizens seems to be expressed by the emphatic words: לבלתי עבד בם ביהודי אחיהו ["that none should serve himself of them, i. e., of a Jew his brother"] v. 9, and לבלתי עבד בם עוד ["that none should serve themselves of them any more"] v. 10.

the celebration of the year of Jubilee, i e., about the time of the destruction of the first monarchy. [1] From this time forward, therefore, fellow-countrymen could only be hired as free workmen, day-laborers, waiters and house servants [2] We find, indeed, that under the despotic rule of Herod the old law, according to which a Hebrew could be sold for theft, was again introduced; the people, how- ever, appear to have resisted the execution of this ordinance by refusing to buy such slaves, whence the King caused thieves to be sold into foreign countries; but by this proceeding he only exasperated the people still more. [3]

Regarding those Hebrews who had, either through war or in any other way, fallen into servitude among heathens, it was at all times considered as a most sacred duty, resting upon every Hebrew who possessed the means, to ransom them. [4]

II.—THE CONDITION OF SLAVES WHO WERE NOT HEBREWS.

§ 14.

a. *Whence Were those Slaves usually Obtained?*

The real slaves whom it was allowed to hold for life might be obtained, accord- ing to the Mosaic law (Levit. xxv. 44–46), partly from among the surrounding nations, partly from among the strangers and foreign settlers in the country, but not from among the Canaanitish peoples who dwelt originally in the land, because these nations, who were deeply dyed in vice and idolatry, were to be utterly ex- tirpated, in order that all temptation might be removed from the immigrating Israelites (Cf. Deut. xx, 16–19). But as these nations were never actually rooted out of the country, many of them having remained within the dominions of the Israelites (Cf. Judges i, 28, sqq.) it was natural that most of the slaves should, at a later period be obtained from among these very *Canaanites*. And in this fact we may find the reason why the Rabbis ordinarily employ the words עבד כנעני " Canaanitish slave," as the designation for any slave who was not a Hebrew. [5]

§ 15.

b. *How Were Such Slaves Originally Acquired ?*

There were three ways in which heathen slaves were originally acquired :

1. By *purchase, i. e.*, by buying from the nations mentioned above partly slaves of their own, partly prisoners of war, and probably to some extent also, children who were sold by their parents because of their poverty. This was probably the

---

1 אין עבד עברי נוהג אלא בזמן שהיובל נוהג, Kidushin 63 and Erachin 29; Cf. also Maimond. Abadim i, 10 and Jobel ushemita x, 8 and 9.

2 שמעי, שמש, שכיר, פעל.

3 Cf. Josephus Antiqq. xvi, 1, 1.

4 Nehem. v. 8; Cf. also Baba bathra fol. 8: פדיון שבוים מצוה רבה.

5 It is possible that with this term the Rabbis also intended to designate the *real, perma- nent* slave in contradistinction to the Hebrew servant, *who was not in the proper sense of the word a slave*, so that כנעני is an allusion to Gen. ix. 25, where Canaan is cursed as the "*ser- vant of servants*," i. e., as the meanest of all slaves: vid. Rashi on Kidushin 22b: כל עברים נקראי׳׳ם על שם כנען משום דכתיב ביה עבד עברים

most common method of obtaining them, and such slaves are in the Scriptures often called מקנת כסף slaves "*bought with money*" (see Gen. xvii. 12, 13, 23, 27), in order to distinguish them from those "born in the house."

2. By *contract, i. e.*, when individual strangers, who dwelt in the land and were unable to maintain themselves by free labor, entered voluntarily, either for a specified period of time or forever into the state of slavery in order thus to be relieved from the necessity of caring for their own support.

3. By *conquest in war,* [1] *i. e.*, when those prisoners of war who were either taken on the field of battle or at the conquest of hostile cities were deprived of their liberty and made slaves by the conquerors. *The stealing of men by violence or kidnapping*, a very common method of obtaining slaves among the ancient nations, was regarded by the Hebrews as so heinous a crime, that when the person thus stolen was a fellow-countryman, it was, like murder, punished with death (Exod. xxi. 16, Deut. xxiv. 7).

A very considerable increase of the number of slaves was, however, obtained in the children who were born of bondwoman in contubernal unions, and who, as "children of the bondwoman," or as "born in the house," were the serfs of the master. These were, from the earliest times, regarded as the best and most trust-worthy, because they had grown up in the family and were familiar with all the affairs of the household, so that their fidelity and attachment could be more certainly reckoned upon (Gen. xiv. 14).

§ 16.

c. *Number and Price of these Slaves.*

In the absence of all definite accounts it is impossible to ascertain exactly how great the number of these slaves was at different times among the Hebrews. That this number was, at all events, very small in comparison with the vast hosts of slaves among the Greeks and Romans, [2] may be inferred from divers circumstances. An excess of slaves presupposed, at all times, an extensive traffic in slaves and regular slave-markets. But of neither of these is any trace to be discovered among the Hebrews. [3]

---

1 In the Mishna Kidushin i, 3, the three modes of obtaining Canaanitish slaves are designated by the words : בכסף בשטר ובחזקה, which may be regarded as corresponding with the three methods of obtaining them described above as *purchase, contract* and *conquest in war.* In reality, however, the Mishna at the place referred to, treats, not of the *original* acquisition of slaves, but only of the manner in which, in a transfer of property, the mastership over [or right in] slaves is just as in the case of other kinds of property, assumed by means either of *money*, or of *contract*, or of *actual appropriation* (i. e., by requiring the services of the slave).

2 Athenæus states the number of slaves in Attica alone to have been 400,000, in Corinth 450,000, and in the small island of Ægina 470,000. In Rome, under the empire, many a rich citizen had alone from 10,000 to 20,000 slaves.

3 The Mishna first mentions the sale of slaves in the market. Cf. Baba Kama viii. 1: עבד הנמכר בשוק ; but even this does not presuppose an extensive slave trade carried on in markets expressly arranged for this traffic. The expression occurring in the Siphra, upon Levit. xxv. 42, אבן הלקח (Cf. also Maimon. Abad. 1, 5), to designate the stone elevation, upon which the slaves to be publicly sold were placed, refers probably only to the practice which is known to have prevailed in Rome at the sale of slaves : cf. the expression, "de lapide emtus," Cic. in Pis. 15.

It is only in the account of the return from the Babylonian captivity that a statement occurs from which we may derive a proximate estimate of the numerical proportion of the slaves to the free Hebrews. According to Ezra ii. 64, 65 and Nehem. vii. 67, there were in the train of the 42,360 returning exiles 7,337 slaves of both sexes. This gave, on an average, only one slave to every five or six free persons, and, as the latter is precisely the average number of persons in a family, one slave to each family. It is probable that in the different periods of the Jewish history this was the normal numerical proportion. It is to be presumed that the more wealthy and powerful families employed, at times, a greater number of slaves for the raising of cattle, the cultivation of the soil, and the different domestic occupations; but then the poorer families often had none at all (Prov. xii. 9), or several families were sometimes satisfied with having one slave in common, who served the several families in turn on certain fixed days. [1] We know that during the time of the second temple no slaves at all were held either by the Essenes or the Therapeutæ; for those sects repudiated every species of slavery as incompatible with the natural equality of all human beings. [2] The Pharisees also were, from moral considerations, opposed at least to the holding of many slaves, and recommended that in domestic service poor Hebrews should be employed rather than slaves. [3]

The price of slaves was, of course, different at different times, and was conformed moreover to the age, sex, health, strength, capacity and skill of individual slaves. We learn from Exod. xxi. 32, where the restitution to be made for a slave who had been killed by an unruly ox occurs, that the average price of a common laboring slave of either sex amounted to thirty shekels. If, as many suppose, the normal price of slaves was really made the basis of the census recorded in Levit. xxvii. 8-10, then this price varied, according to the sex and age of the slave from five shekels to fifty, and—slaves—brought the highest price between the ages of twenty and sixty, while female slaves brought less than male slaves. With reference to the later times of the Jewish Commonwealth, Josephus [4] reports the ransom paid for an Israelitish captive at 120 drachmæ (about $21.18), which was probably at the time the average value of a slave. As the value of the shekel was, in later times, equal to four Attic drachmæ (i. e., a little over sixty-eight cents), [5] we would thus again have the sum of thirty shekels, only that these shekels exceeded those of the days of Moses in weight.

§ 17.

d. The Legal Position of Slaves.

Although the position which the law of Moses gave the heathen slave was essentially different from that of the Hebrew servant, as the latter was to belong to the master only for a fixed period and was to be regarded by him only as a hired servant, while the former could be held as property in perpetuo and trans-

---

1 Cf. the case repeatedly considered in the Talmudic law: עבד של שני שותפין
2 Philo Opp. editio Mangey ii. 458 and 482.
3 Vide Mishnah Aboth ii. 8 and i. 5; Cf. also Baba Mezia 60 b.
4 Antiq. xii. 2, 3.
5 Antiq. iii. 8, 2.

mitted as such to heirs (Levit. xxv. 46), nevertheless this position was far more favorable than with any other nation of antiquity. It is well known that among the other nations the slave was in the eye of the law, nothing more than a chattel, devoid of all personality, so that the master might do with him what he pleased, and even put him to death; [1] among the Hebrews, on the contrary, the slave was regarded as being indeed the property of the master, not, however, as a *chattel* but as a *person*. The fact is that he was only so far regarded as property that the master could, as his purchaser, claim all that he produced and earned; inasmuch, however, as the slave could never cease to be a *man*, he was looked upon as a *person* possessing certain natural human rights, with which the master even could not with impunity interfere.

When considered from this point of view, the statements both of the Bible and the Rabbis regarding the legal position of slaves become perfectly clear. Regarded as the master's property, the slave could again be sold or transferred to an heir, bestowed as a present or given in pledge [2] by the master. When viewed as a person, however, his life, his health and soundness of limb constituted an inviolable possession to which the power of the master did not extend. And although therefore the latter could not, by means of corporeal chastisement, force him to labor, he was at liberty to employ milder disciplinary measures. The direct killing of a slave, even when his death was the effect of chastisement with a cane or rod, was to be punished (Exod. xxi. 20), i. e , according to the explanation of the Rabbis, it was to be expiated by the execution of the master. [3] If the death of the slave did not ensue immediately upon the inflicted chastisement, but after several days, so that the chastisement could not be regarded with certainty as the cause of his death, the mas er was not to be punished, as the loss of his slave was then considered a sufficient punishment (ibid. v. 21). But if the master had, in chastising his slave, made use of an instrument which was obviously such as that a blow given with it would prove mortal, the master was punished with death, although the slave had not died until some time after he had received the injury. If a man knocked out an eye or only a tooth of his servant, or inflicted a serious injury on any part of his body, which could not then be restored to its normal condition, [4] the servant obtained his liberty immediately (Exod. xxi, 21, 26, 27).

In so far as the slave was the property of his master, he could earn or acquire nothing for himself. In this respect the principle obtained, " the hand of the slave is the hand of the master," [5] or, what the slave acquires, he acquires for the

---

1 Vide Heineccius Ant. Rom. I, Tit III, 2, on the subject of Roman slaves: non pro personis, sed pro rebus, immo pro nullis habebantur, etc. (" they were regarded, not as persons, but as things, aye, even as not anything at all.") Cf. also Gai. Inst. I. 52. Apud omnes peræque gentes animadvertere possumus, dominis in servos vitæ necisque protestatem esse ı " We may perceive equally among all nations that masters have the power of life and death over their slaves)".

2 The giving of a slave in pledge did not, however, afford the creditor perfect security, as the debtor could give the slave whom he had pledged his liberty: Cf. Mishna Gittin IV, 4.

3 Cf. Maimon. " concerning murder," II, 14.

4 Vide Kid: 24, where 24 such parts of the body are specified, such as the ears, fingers, toes, etc.

5 יד עבד כיד רבו Baba Mezia 96. Kidushin 23b.

master." To the master, therefore, belonged, not only whatsover the slave had acquired by his labor, or found, or received as a present, but he was also entitled to indemnification for injuries which the slave had suffered in his person at the hands of others. [1]

Regarded as a person the slave was responsible for his own acts. If, therefore, he had injured other persons, the master was not under legal obligation to make restitution; on the contrary, the restitution which the law prescribed in such cases now rested upon the slave, and he was bound to make it after he obtained his liberty. [2]

In his relation to third persons the criminal law regarded the slave as being on precisely the same footing as the free Israelite. The premeditated murder of a slave was punished with death, whoever slew him unintentionally, was exiled to one of the cities of refuge; and conversely, murder committed by the slave was punished in precisely the same manner. [3] A third person who either wounded, beat or defamed a slave, was liable to the same penalties as if he had inflicted these injuries upon a free Israelite. [4]

§ 18.

e. *The Religious and Civil Position of the Slave.*

The sacred law expressly requires that the master shall let his non-Hebrew [foreign] slave participate in the three most significant sacred rites of the Israelitish nation :

1. In circumcision, the sign of the covenent. According to this command slaves born in the house were to receive this sign of the covenant on the eighth day after they were born, and purchased slaves, when they entered the service of a Hebrew master. Gen. xvii. 10–14; Exod. xii, 44.

2. In the observance of the Sabbath. Both the male and the female slave were, equally with the master, forbidden to labor on the Sabbath, and required to enjoy the rest of that day (Exod. xx. 10, xxiii. 12; Deut. v. 14).

3. In eating the pascal lamb, and in the rejoicings connected with the sacrificial rites of the other festivals (Exod. xii. 44; Deut. xii. 18, xvi. 11, 14).

By his participation in these three sacred rites the slave passed out of heathenism and was, in a measure, regarded as a fellow-believer. [5] He could not, how-

---

1 מה שקנה עבד קנה רבו Pes. 88*b*. The Roman law expresses the same principle in almost precisely the same words: Quodcunque per servum acquiritur id domi o acquiritur. ["What-ever is acquired by the slave is acquired for the master"]. Gai. Inst. I. 52.

2 Mishna Baba Kama viii. 4; Cf. also Mishna Jedaim iv, 7. and Maim. "Concerning Theft," i. 9.

3 Maimon. "Concerning Murder," ii. 10–14.

4 Mishna Baba Kama viii. 3, Maccoth fol. 9 a; Cf. Maimon. Hilch. Chobel umazik iii. 4 and 10. This was different in the Roman law, according to which what was slander or defamation in respect of a free citizen, was not likewise such as regarded a slave. It was also allowed to revile the slaves of others and to strike them with the fist with impunity; Cf. Gai. iii. 222. "Si quis servo convicium fecerit, vel pugno eum percusserit, non proponitur ulla formula; nec temere petenti datur." (If any one has gathered a crowd round (mobbed) a slave, or struck him with his fist, there is no mode of proceeding prescribed, nor is there any immediate redress to a plaintiff).

5 אח הוא במצות Baba Kama 88; Sanhedr. 86; Cf. also Maim. "Concerning Murder," II 11.

ever, he looked upon as a full participant of the religious and national covenant, [1] because as such he would have ceased to be a real slave. Under no circumstances could a foreigner enter into the covenant of faith without voluntary choice, which could not be looked for in a slave.

Other religious duties the law of Moses does not expressly enjoin upon the slave. The Rabbis, however, assert that upon him rested those religious obligations also, which were binding equally upon the female and the male sex; [2] and this opinion is based upon the circumstance that, whereas the slave was required to renounce idolatry and all idolatrous practices, the injunction to perform those religious duties afforded him the means of satisfying his religious wants. But how far the Rabbis were from proposing to do violence in any respect to the conscience of the slave, appears plainly from their so interpreting the law that the purchased slave was not even to be compelled to submit to circumcision, although his receiving that rite was especially commanded by the law. If, therefore, the slave refused to submit to the rite, the master was to wait patiently a whole year, and to endeavor, by kind admonitions, to bring him to a better mind. If, however, his efforts then remained fruitless, he was obliged to sell him again to a heathen. But if the slave had at the very commencement of his servitude made the omission of circumcision a condition of his entering the master's service, then the latter was at liberty to keep him, though uncircumcised, for ever. [3] The slave who had once been removed out of heathenism by means of circumcision, could not again be sold to a heathen or into a foreign land, because he might thus be easily led to relapse into heathenism. If the master, nevertheless, sold him, he could, under certain circumstances, be compelled to buy him back again; and in that event he was not allowed to retain him in his service, but had to let him go free. [4]

Before the magistrates the evidence of a slave was of no avail. This arose probably from the unfavorable opinion which was generally entertained respecting the moral character of slaves. [5] The Rabbis, however, recognize in this exclusion only a consequence of the circumstance that, according to Talmudic law, the entire female sex was also excluded from giving evidence before court, and that hence it was inadmissible to place slaves higher than the female sex, who were full participants in the national and religious covenant of Israel. [6]

Neither a male nor a female slave had the capacity of contracting a valid marriage. [7] If the master permitted a bondman to cohabit with a bondwoman, this connexion was not looked upon as marriage. Hence the master was at liberty to let the same bondwoman afterwards live in a contubernal union with another slave. [8] But this was not done by noble-minded masters, who gave

---

1 Baba Kama ibid; Cf. also Sanhedrin 58b. רככר ישראל רא בא.

2 Chagiga 4; Nazir 61; Kerithoth 7.

3 Jebamoth, 48 b.

4 Gittin, 43 b. Maimon Abadim viii. 1.

5 משום פריצותא Kethub 11; עברא בהפקירא ניחא ליה Aboth II. 7; מירבה עברים מרבה גזי Pesachim 91.

6 Baba Kama 88. Cf. also Maim. "Concerning Evidence," IX. 4.

7 לא תפסי בהו קידושין Jebamoth 45 a; Kidushin 68.

8 Cf. Maim. Issure biah XIV. 19.

the bondwoman exclusively to the s'ave to whom she had been originally assigned. [1]

Children who were the fruit of the illicit intercourse of a free man with a bondwoman were held as slaves, and belonged as such to the master of the mother; children, however, whom a bondman had with a free woman were, although esteemed ignoble regarded as free born; for in such cases the child always shared the condition of the mother. [2]

The seduction of a maid-servant betrothed to another man, [3] but not yet set quite free, was, according to the law of Moses punished with scourging, but not, as in the case of a betrothed free maiden, with death. Besides this the seducer had to atone for his sin by bringing a trespass offering (Levit. xix. 20–22).

f. Domestic Condition.

§ 19.

(1) Employment of the Slaves.

The employment of the slaves differed according to their various abilities and capacities and the wants of their owner. The male slaves were probably employed chiefly in agriculture and the breeding of cattle, the two principal occupations of the nation. They did the harder work of the household, and waited upon the person of the master at table, in dressing and undressing, washing and anointing him. When the master went into the bath it was usual for a slave to follow him and carry his garments. With such personal attendance upon the master the slave usually began his term of service. [4] Slaves were apparently, not much employed in mechanical pursuits, as these were highly esteemed by the Hebrews, and doubtless carried on chiefly by free men. The Rabbis, however, make mention also of slaves employed in trade and mechanical occupations, such as keepers of public baths, barbers, bakers and the like. [5]

Skilful and trustworthy slaves were not only sometimes employed as overseers of the other slaves and as domestic stewards (Gen. xv. 2, xxiv. 2; II. Sam. ix. 10), but seem even to have been appointed governors to the sons of the house (Prov. xvii. 2). The female slaves who were under the immediate authority of the mistress of the family were expected to render her the same personal services as the male slaves performed for the master. Besides these they attended to the female occupations of the house, the principal of which were baking, cooking, grinding, washing and spinning. They were employed as nurses and as maids to take care of children. The hardest labor that female slaves were required to perform consisted in preparing grain for baking, which was done by means of hand-

---

1 Cf. Nidda 47.

2 Maimon. Abad. IX. 1–3; Issure biah XV. 3, 4. The same principle was held by the Roman law: qui nascitur sine legitimo matrimonio, matrem sequitur ("he that is born out of lawful wedlock follows the condition of the mother)." Cf. Gai. I. 82.

3 With reference to the different interpretations of this statute Cf. Talmud Kerith 11a.

4 Cf. Kidushin 22b.

5 Cf. Mechiltha on Exod. xxi. 2 and Siphra on Levit. xxv. 39, where it is maintained that it was forbidden to employ Hebrew servants in such money-making pursuits.

mills (Job xxxi. 10; Is. xlvii. 2; Cf. also Exod. xi. 5 and Eccles. xii. 3). The lowest position was that of those female slaves whose duty it was to wait upon the master's male slaves (I. Sam. xxv. 41), and with whom they were made to cohabit. The only outdoor work in which maid-servants appear to have been employed was the binding of sheaves (Cf. Ruth ii. 8, 9, 23).

§ 20.

(2) Treatment of Slaves.

The enactment of the Mosaic law, which required that both male and female slaves should enjoy a weekly day of rest, was itself sufficient to secure them against being overtasked with excessive labor. The statute also by which it is enjoined that animals shall not be tasked beyond their strength, and which, therefore, forbids that animals of unequal strength shall labor together in the same yoke (Deut. xxii. 10) conveyed a forcible appeal for so much the greater consideration to be shown for the physical ability of slaves to labor. Above all, however, the ever cherished recollection of the heavy burdens borne by the people as slaves in Egypt from which divine mercy, in punishing their oppressors, had delivered them, as also the admonitions to deal kindly and mercifully with all strangers and destitute persons, which the divine law reiterated with direct reference to these reminiscences, could not fail to have an important influence upon the treatment of slaves. We can therefore look upon it as certain, that, as a general thing, the condition of slaves was among the Hebrews far more tolerable and favorable than among any other nation of antiquity. Several passages in the proverbs of Solomon (xxix. 19, 21) and of Sirah (xxxiii. 25–29), which caution against the excessive indulgence of slaves, especially the younger ones, give rise to the presumption that most unhappy effects had not been infrequently experienced in consequence of too great tenderness and indulgence in the treatment of slaves. Disobedient and indolent slaves were, doubtless, sometimes chastised with a cane or rod, and even, in cases of extraordinary contumacy, put in chains (Sirach xxxiii. 29), but the severe penalties mentioned above, as annexed to the killing or serious maiming of a slave, could not fail to tie the hands of a hard-hearted master, and to restrain him from allowing chastisement to degenerate into cruelty. Of the inhuman modes of punishment which were employed among the Romans for even slight offenses, [1] not a trace can be discovered among the Hebrews.

To the kindness with which slaves were, in general, treated, we must also ascribe the circumstance that not a single instance of such servile insurrections as were not infrequent among the Romans and Greeks, is known to have occurred among the Hebrews. Instances even of slaves running away from their masters appear to have been very rare; at all events, there is only a solitary case of this kind, that of two of the servants of the violent Shimei (1 Kings ii. 39), recorded in the Bible. [2]

If thus the treatment of slaves was, as a general thing, kind and humane, noble-minded masters distinguished themselves pre-eminently in this respect.

---

1 Cf. Becker's Gallus, i, 129 sqq.

2 From the time of the Talmud several cases are recorded Gittin 45.

Thus Job, when reviewing his past life with reference to its moral character, was able to bear witness concerning himself, that he had never despised the cause of his man-servant or his maid-servant, nor had, in general, at any time forgotten that in the dignity of human nature the slave was his equal (Job xxxi. 13–15). The opulent and highly respected Boaz enters with a truly paternal affability the circle of his *laboring slaves*, and is the first to offer them the salutation : " The Lord be with you " (Ruth ii. 4). The Talmud makes frequent mention of distinguished men of later times, and reports that they gave their servants a portion of every dish of which they themselves partook, and that they even had their food served up to them before they themselves sat down to their meals ; [1] that they received condolences on account of the death of a faithful slave, just as when a near relation had died, and that they addressed aged slaves with the honorable appellative of *father N.*, or *mother N.* [2] A distinguished rabbi even proposed the general introduction of the practice of chanting publicly at the funerals of virtuous slaves the customary lament : " Woe ! the good, faithful man, productive of good was his activity." [3]

Also in their conduct toward the slaves of others the Hebrews observed the duties and performed the kind offices dictated by philanthropy. To calumniate a slave to his master was looked upon as an execrable sin which God will not leave unpunished (Prov. xxx. 10). Those who are wont in any relation to practice beneficence and mercy were equally conscientious in practicing them toward slaves, [4] and as it was the duty of every man to ransom a free man who had fallen into captivity, so also was this duty recognized with regard to a slave who had been taken prisoner. [5]

Faithful slaves not infrequently, especially at the death of their master, obtained their liberty as a reward of their faithful services, and in that event usually received a part of the inheritance (Prov. xvii. 2). In default of male heirs the chief of the slaves or house-steward was in the earliest times, sometimes adopted as a son and appointed sole heir (Gen. xv. 3), or married to the master's daughter (1 Chron. ii. 34), in order that thus the property might be kept together. The latter alternative was sometimes also adopted under other circumstances : for example, if the daughters of the house could not get any free-born husbands ; at any rate, there was a proverb indicating this circumstance current in Jerusalem : " If your daughter is marriageable, emancipate your slave and let him become her husband." [6] Female slaves, on the contrary, were not made entirely free unless they were demanded by some person in marriage, as it would otherwise have been no kindness to them to give them their liberty, for they were likely thus to be cast entirely unprotected upon the world. When therefore it was proposed to reward a female slave for faithful services, it was often considered more judicious merely to take her out of her low position and to retain her for the performance of the lighter labors of the family. [7]

---

1 Ketbub 61 and Talmud Jerus. Baba Kama 6.
2 Berachoth 16b.
3 Berachoth ibid
4 Cf. Gittin 12a.
5 Cf. Gittin 37b.
6 Pesachim 113a.
7 Cf. Gittin 40a.

§ 21.

g. *The Emancipation of Slaves.*

The law of Moses makes no provision for the emancipation of slaves who were not Hebrews, except in the case of the slave who had received some serious bodily injury at the hands of his master (Exod. xxi, 26, 27). But that it presupposes the possibility of his obtaining his liberty under other circumstances also is evident from Levit. xix. 29. These circumstances and the particular manner in which the emancipation was effected, are more fully stated by the rabbis as follows:

1. *Emancipation in consideration of a ransom paid for him.* As the slave, as such, could own no property, his being ransomed was entirely out of the question, unless some third person paid the master the value of the slave, for the purpose of giving him his liberty. This he accordingly received at the very moment when the master acccepted the proffered sum, without any written document being required. [1]

2. *By a certificate of his discharge,* which the master delivered to the slave with his own hands, in the presence of witnesses, or if the certificate had been signed by witnesses, by the hands of a third person. The phraseology of such certificates might vary as, *e. g.,* " Thou art now a free man," or " Thou belongest now to thyself," or it might be worded in some other way, provided only that in it the master distinctly renounced his claim to the slave, and in no manner whatever reserved to himself any right to him. [2]

3. *By Testament, i. e.,* if the master in his last will and testament declared the slave to be free, or either required or requested his heir to emancipate him. [3]

4. Lastly, *by tacit emancipation,* [4] *i. e.,* if the master indicated in any way whatever, that he no longer regarded the slave as such, if *e. g.,* he constituted him heir of his entire property, [5] or gave him a free-born woman to wife, or if he numbered him among ten free Hebrews selected as participants in some sacred rite, or in a word, if he ordered him to perform any act which only a free Hebrew was required to perform. [6] In all these cases the slave at once obtained his freedom, but in order to render this perfectly valid, a certificate of emancipation was requisite, which the master could be compelled to execute. [7]

Over slaves whom he had emancipated the Hebrew master did not, as was the case among the Romans and Greeks, afterwards exercise any patronage; much less was he allowed to reduce him again to the condition of a slave, if he repented of having emancipated him. [8] After he had obtained his liberty the

---

1 Maimon. Abadin, V. 2.

2 Maimon. Abad. V., 3, and VII., 1,

3 Maimon. ibid VI., 4 and Sechija umathana IX., 11.

4 Similar to the Roman manumissio per mensam, just as the two preceding modes of emancipation correspond with the Roman manumissio per epistolam and per testamentum.

5 Mishna Peah III., 8.

6 Gittin fol. XXXIX., 40.

7 Maimon. Abad. VIII., 17.

8 Maimon. ib'd.

slave was required to receive in open day, and in the presence of three Hebrews, the ritual bath which was in Judaism practiced in connection with the reception of proselytes, [1] and was then regarded as in every respect a full member of the national and religious covenant of the Israelites. [2]

22.

The Influence of the Legislation of Moses upon the Condition of Slaves among the Neighboring People.

The example of the kind treatment which slaves received among the Hebrews was itself sufficient to exert an ennobling influence upon the surrounding peoples in their treatment of their slaves, and there is really no evidence that among these peoples the condition of slaves was, as a general thing, as deplorable as it was among the Greeks and the Romans at the height of their civilization. But among the laws of Moses there was one that had been enacted for the benefit of foreign slaves, and which could not fail to be eminently efficacious in this particular. According to Deut. xxiii. 16, 17, no slave who had escaped from his master and had taken refuge in the dominions of the Israelites, could, under any circumstances, be delivered up to his master or taken as a slave. He might, on the contrary, settle as a free man in the land in whatever place he choose, and was entitled to all civil rights, which the law guaranteed to the freeborn foreigner. If the slaves of surrounding peoples could thus without difficulty escape from harsh treatment, and, in fact, from slavery altogether, their masters must, of course, have exerted themselves so as to gain their attachment by clemency and kindness, that their slaves would not be tempted to seek their liberty and the recognition of their rights as men, in a land where these were guaranteed by a sacred law.

---

1 Jebamoth fol. 47; Issure biah XIII., 12.
2 Maimon. Issure biah XII., 17.

MAIDEN.   MATRON.

COSTUMES OF ANCIENT HEBREWS.

www.ingramcontent.com/pod-product-compliance
Lightning Source LLC
Chambersburg PA
CBHW030915260626
47169CB00008B/2865